The Tay Bridge Tragedy

by
Dennis Hamley

Illustrations by George Buchanan

W
FRANKLIN WATTS
NEW YORK • LONDON • SYDNEY

1

Bad dreams

Alastair Reid pressed his face to the window of the railway carriage. Outside was deep darkness. The rough horsehair of the seats scratched and tickled him. The gas lamps hummed and hissed and sometimes flickered so much they nearly went out. He shivered with the cold. Only the first-class passengers would have footwarmers on this bitter night. Underneath he could hear the wheelbeats – thud-thud-thud, thud-thud-thud – as the

six-wheeled coaches jolted over the track. The engine whistle screamed. Steam and smoke drifted past the window like strange grey ghosts in the blackness.

Alastair imagined the fireman stoking the red-hot fire and the driver peering out into the dark.

The wind howled. It blew like the breath of a furious giant determined to blast them off the rails. It slammed into the sides of the train.

But still the train butted forward.

There were lights far below, as if the

railway had left the ground and was
climbing through the air. The sight made
Alastair dizzy. For what seemed a lifetime,
the train inched forward into nothing. The
wind's roar grew and grew until it
drowned even the wheelbeats and the
engine noise. The carriage shook from side
to side, almost toppling over. They seemed
to go into a cage, and passed girders and
iron pillars which took away a little of the
dizziness – but none of the terror. Strange,

echoing clangs and groans reached into
the coach.

Then, suddenly, it was over. Wheelbeats,
screeching, sparks – they were all gone.
There was a final deafening blast from the
wind, then a violent blow from the side as if
the giant, impatient to finish things, had hit
the train with his fist.

Alastair heard a terrible, echoing,
rasping clang of uprooting metal – then
they were free, really flying, twisting,

turning through the air. All the gas lamps went out and the dangerous smell of unburnt coal-gas filled his nose.

He flew out of his seat, turned over in the air like a seal in the sea and found himself sitting on the ceiling. The windows broke and crumpled like paper. Cold, dirty, choking water surged in and Alastair felt it cover him, reach his chin, his nose, his eyes ...

★ ★ ★ ★

Alastair woke. He was still shivering. Usually he couldn't remember his dreams, but every detail of this one stayed in his mind.

Where had it come from? He got out of bed and opened his curtains. He looked out of the window of his parent's house in Magdalen Green, Dundee, and surveyed the broad River Tay in front of him. It was a fine, still, frosty Christmas Eve. The year was 1879. A plume of white smoke showed

where a train of the North British Railway was crossing the wonderful new bridge across the Tay to start the long journey to Edinburgh and London.

Alastair was twelve. He had been only eleven when the bridge had opened in 1878. What a fanfare there had been! What pride everybody took in this great work! And it was a great work. Queen Victoria herself, on a memorable day, had

crossed it in a special train and had knighted Thomas Bouch, designer of the great Tay Bridge.

Wonderful. Two miles long. The longest bridge in the world. And the best.

So everybody said. And yet ...

Alastair watched the train out of the window. It moved slowly round the curve where the single track, balanced on those slim, spidery pillars, turned to face Wormit Hill and St Fort station on the south side. Soon it would leave that unprotected run which made him dizzy even to look at and

be surrounded by the high girders in the middle of the river. The whole thing looked so frail to him, the pillars and piers so thin, the lattice girders so insubstantial. Where were the great plate girders and stone piles of other bridges? 'Muscle without flesh,' someone had said about the Tay Bridge. These thin lattice girders were supposed to be as strong as anything Mr Brunel or Mr Stephenson ever built.

But it didn't look strong to Alastair,

and he knew that there were railwaymen who had seen things they had been told to keep quiet about.

So what about his dream? Was it a premonition? Was it telling him of things which would happen if there was a

great storm?

His father was a railway engineer. He had been working on a new line in Australia and was coming home in time for Hogmanay. A journey from the other side of the world, ending by crossing the bridge. Was his dream about that crossing? Was it a warning?

★ ★ ★ ★

2

Storm

Christmas was three days gone. On Sunday, 28th December, all was quiet and peaceful. The people of Dundee were at church or chapel. The River Tay shimmered in winter sunshine. The Tay Bridge stretched across, silvery in the light, as if a spider had changed his mind and spun his web straight instead of in a circle.

At 1.15pm the little ferry steamer, the *Dundee*, crossed the river to Newport on the south side. Three hundred miles further south, the express train of the Great Northern Railway carrying Alastair's father home was long out of King's Cross and nearing Doncaster. In the house on Magdalen Green, Alastair

and his mother began counting the hours.

Late in the afternoon, a fresh breeze blew up. The cold began to chill bones and make people shiver under heavy coats as they trudged the streets home. In the evening, the *Dundee*, steaming back from Newport, butted its way through water which grew more and more choppy.

"We're in for a storm," said the captain. The passengers knew what he

meant. Storms could blow in from the North Sea and up the River Tay from nowhere, with sudden, frightening violence.

Now it was dark. The navigation lights, strung out all along the bridge, were like a shining necklace, fragile and pretty.

From his upstairs window, Alastair could see them. They seemed to shake as the wind blew stronger. It moaned in the chimney and whined through cracks in the window-frames. He remembered his dream and thought of his father. He would have got off the train at Edinburgh by now and be sailing in the ferry across the Firth of Forth to Burntisland, where the Dundee train would be waiting. Would the gale be as strong there?

Suddenly, he wanted to be with his father. Something dreadful was going to happen. He couldn't stay here shut up in his own house, just waiting. He had to do something.

He called his mother. "I'm going down to the station to wait for the train."

"It's not in for ages yet," she answered. "You're not to go out on a night like this."

Too late. Alastair had pulled on his coat and scarf and opened the front door.

The wind nearly knocked him over. He screwed up his eyes and looked at the bridge. Most of the navigation lights had blown out. Other, dimmer, lights, moved slowly over the bridge. A local train was crossing the river towards the north bank.

A shameful thought entered his mind. If only this train would be blown off the bridge as it collapsed. Then the passengers from Edinburgh couldn't cross it and his father would be safe. No, that was an awful thing to think. Who said the bridge would collapse? It was only a dream.

He was near the station. Where the
Tay Bridge ended, the railway curved into
a cutting lined with grey bricks. There
were no engines at the station, and, he
saw with horror, no glass roof either.
Above the wind's howl he heard a clanging
smash as the wind blew another glass
panel out.

He'd better get to
the station quickly. He
rushed to the entrance
and down the steps, just
in time to see the station
master coming up.

"Go away," he
shouted. "I'm closing
this station entrance."

"But it's me, Mr
Smith."

The station master looked hard at him. "Why, it's young Alastair," he said.

"My father's coming home. He's on the train from Edinburgh. I've come early to meet him."

"It's not safe on the station. Go home."

"But then there'll be nobody to meet him."

Mr Smith thought for a moment. "All right," he said at last. "Your father's a good friend and a railwayman. Join the few passengers who've ventured out. You'll find them sheltering in the waiting-room. And don't come out or you *will* go home."

"Thanks, Mr Smith."

The platform was piled high with broken glass. Alastair picked his way through. In the waiting-room, by the light of the flickering gas lamps, a few huddled passengers waited. The local train finally puffed into the station from its slow journey across the bridge. Before the passengers left the room to join the train on its journey back south, the wind

suddenly shrieked between the walls of the cutting, along the platform and into the waiting room like a mad monster. A woman passenger dropped to her knees, sobbing. "Oh, Lord above, why do I have to travel tonight?" she wailed.

The waiting room door opened. Mr Smith poked his head round. "The train south is waiting," he yelled.

The passengers forced themselves across the platform to the waiting carriages. The guard waved his green flag. The little

engine slowly drew out, its steam swirling
and disappearing in the wind. Alastair
and Mr Smith watched it draw away
towards the bridge. As it met the full
force of the wind outside the cutting,
sparks from its wheels showered in the air
like fireworks.

Mr Smith looked at his big watch.
"Ten to six," he shouted to Alastair.
Alastair heard and nodded. His
father's train was due in just over an hour.

★ ★ ★ ★

3

Journey's end

Donald Reid sat on the train from Edinburgh as it ploughed through the gale. He was nearly home, at last, after a year and a half away and a long journey from the other side of the world. He was so looking forward to seeing his family and

friends and celebrating a proper Scottish Hogmanay. Also, he was really pleased to be crossing the great new Tay Bridge for the first time. When he had left for Australia, it was still being built. But as he looked out of the window and saw the force of the wind, he was not so pleased. He had seen things happening during its construction that he, as a trained engineer, had worried about but had put behind him. They were none of his business.

The ferry crossing over the Firth of Forth was rough. But when he saw the

train waiting at Burntisland, he felt happy.
The locomotive was Number 224, a fine
express engine, only eight years old. The
driver, David Mitchell, and the fireman,
John Marshall, were men he knew well.

Ah, how good it was to be home and
meet people he'd known all his life. He'd
be with his wife again, and with
Alastair, who was only ten when he left.
How the boy must have changed in
eighteen months.

The train's wheels banged along on
the rails and Donald Reid, in spite of the
gale outside, dozed off.

In his dreams he saw Alastair.

★ ★ ★ ★

He woke up suddenly. The train had
stopped. He looked out of the window.
St Fort. Last stop before the bridge. The
ticket collector opened the door of the
compartment. Donald Reid gave up
his ticket.

"It's a rough night," said the ticket
collector.

"Aye, it is that," said Donald. "How's

the bridge faring?"

"The bridge?" replied the ticket collector. "I never cross it."

He left the compartment to go down the rest of the train.

Donald Reid watched him go. That wasn't a very helpful answer. He was stiff from his long journey. He needed a walk. He would ask his good friend, David Mitchell.

Outside on the platform he could hardly stand up. He fought his way up to the engine and the cab, bright and hot with the furnace in the firebox. David Mitchell was leaning out and waiting for the signal.

"How are you, David?" Donald called. "How are things?"

The driver looked down from his cab. "Why, it's Donald Reid," he said. "Welcome home." Then he shouted in Donald's ear, "I'm a wee bit feared for the Tay Bridge. I wish I were safe across that rickety concern."

Donald Reid listened, heard and thought again of Alastair.

★ ★ ★ ★

Five minutes later, station master, porter and ticket collector watched the train slowly draw out. Its red lights dwindled away as it entered the cutting before it came to the bridge.

Six minutes after that, the signalman in the signalbox guarding the south end of the bridge was handing out the baton.

This was a token that every train had to carry to make sure only one train could be crossing the river at any one time.

John Marshall, the fireman, stretched his arm out of the cab to take the baton. He waved and smiled. Then the train set off again, left solid land and moved on to the bridge. Far across the water, the lights of Dundee gleamed, warm and welcoming.

★ ★ ★ ★

4

Waiting

Seven o'clock came. Alastair was alone in the waiting room. All the lights were blown out. The station was a dark, cold place.

The door opened. Mr Smith came in. "The signal's at clear," he said. "Your father's train is on the bridge. He'll be here in a few minutes."

"Can I come out and see the train
crossing the bridge?"
asked Alastair.

"In this wind? No,
you can't. You stay
put," said Mr Smith.

Too late again.
Alastair was outside,
struggling to stand up
against the blast and
fight his way past
more waiting people,
through broken glass to
the very end of the
platform. Here, he
could just see the
rails curving away towards the bridge.

This wasn't good enough. Behind him,
people were talking:

"Where's that train?"

"It's usually across the bridge by now."

"I'm getting worried."

"You don't think...?"

Then somebody said, "Why not telegraph the other side?"

"There's nobody here on Sundays who can work the instruments," said Mr Smith.

"I'll have a go," said Mr Roberts, who was in charge of the engine shed. But after a moment, he said, "It's dead. The line must be down."

Alastair couldn't stand this any more.

Nobody noticed him. He slipped away, off the platform and on to the tracks, scrunching his way through the heavy stone ballast. In the open, the gale was even stronger. But he pressed on until he came to the shelter of the signal box on the north bank. He leant up against the wall and looked out where he could see the bridge curving to the left over the river.

Yes, there were lights on it. They were moving very slowly. The wind tore at Alastair's face. He had to screw his eyes up so he could only half see. So was it only in his imagination that there was a sudden flash and then three bright lights curving downwards like meteors?

He blinked and looked again. There were now no lights at all. Just solid blackness.

No, it couldn't be. He'd had a dream and now there was a bit of a gale, it kept coming back to him. That's all it was. Nothing could really happen to a train full of people on the great Tay Bridge.

Above the wind's scream he heard more scrunching footsteps. Mr Smith and Mr Roberts had arrived. They did not see him but climbed the steps to the signal box.

Alastair waited. What should he do? Go back with them and tell them what he thought he'd seen?

In a few minutes they came down again. But they weren't going back into the station. They were crossing the bridge.

What a terrible thing to try and do. Yet, as Alastair watched them, he knew he would have to go as well.

* * * *

5

Crossing

The bridge shook and swayed under him as
he crawled along the slippery wooden
decking. He clutched at the flimsy handrail.
Far below, he could hear the thunderous
crash of huge waves smashing against the
bridge's piers. Sometimes, the wind gusted so

strongly that he had to kneel, still clutching the handrails. Alastair thought that at any second he would lose his grip and be hurled into the raging waters beneath. Time and time again he nearly gave up. But no, he wouldn't. If something terrible had happened to his father, he must know what it was.

His eyes grew more used to the darkness. He could see the two railwaymen struggling on ahead, gripping the opposite handrail. They had no idea he was behind them. The further they managed to go, the sooner they would see the great high girders of the central section

standing straight and proud in front of them, and they would know their fears were for nothing and the train was safe. Perhaps it had stopped and reversed its way back to the south bank. Perhaps, indeed, it had never left.

Alastair had no idea how long they had been on the bridge. The whole of his life, it seemed by now. But what was happening to Mr Smith? Was he feeling giddy? Alastair didn't believe he was too scared. Yet it looked as though he couldn't go on. He stopped, still clinging to the handrail. Alastair saw him signing to Mr Roberts to go on without him.

Alastair never considered stopping as well. He gritted his teeth, screwed up his courage and battled on. Mr Smith never saw him.

Surely they must have seen the high girders by now.

Suddenly, Mr Roberts stopped. Alastair stopped as well. He blinked, trying to make out what Mr Roberts had seen.

Then he knew. There were no high girders any more. The bridge just stopped, about eight yards in front of them. Two rails poked out straight into empty space. Beyond them was nothing. Just empty air and churning water.

The Tay Bridge was down.

Alastair saw Mr Roberts slowly, daringly, inching a little further forward. He forced himself to do the same. No, the broken rails were not twisted. They were snapped cleanly, as if a giant had risen out of the water and bitten them off.

Far below, the water foamed angrily in the howling wind. Somewhere, deep underneath, was half of a great bridge, one of the wonders of the world, and a whole train of engine and six coaches with forty people trapped and drowned.

And among them was Donald Reid, Alastair's father.

Mr Roberts waited for a moment, absolutely still. Alastair sometimes watched him, sometimes the black, heaving water underneath. At last, Mr Roberts turned and slowly fought his way back. Alastair waited, then, his eyes blinded with tears as well as spray, started on the lonely, dangerous, hopeless journey to the shore.

* * * *

Many people that night thought they saw strange lights on the bridge: showers of sparks, sudden bright flashes, balls of fire falling towards the water. Some, through binoculars, had seen the sight there was no mistaking – the long gap in the river where there should be a bridge. Later in the night, the steamer *Dundee* steamed as close to the bridge as the captain dared. A boat was lowered and the crew rowed it along the whole gap. They found

wreckage, broken girders, wooden planking. But they found no train and no bodies. Yet there was no doubt. The train was lost. A long time would pass before its remains were found.

★ ★ ★ ★

6

Homecoming

Someone ran to Alastair's house to fetch his mother. When he was brought off the bridge, she put her arms round his shaking body and took him home. Then she boiled water for a hot bath for him. She was too thankful to see her son alive to be angry.

What must have happened to her husband had not yet sunk in.

When Alastair was warm and dry she put him to bed. Neither said a single word, and when Alastair was asleep she stood all night looking out of the front window at the ruined bridge. As light came and the wind died, she saw clearly the empty river and knew there could be no doubt.

At ten o'clock in the morning, the minister from the church called. He offered Alastair and his mother his deepest sympathy and suggested they say prayers together. So they all knelt in the living room and, as the minister droned on, Alastair found himself reliving last night's terrible moments.

From outside came the clip-clop of a horse's hooves and the rumble of a cab's wheels. They seemed to stop outside the house.

Suddenly, there was a loud rat-a-tat at the front door. Mrs Reid looked up.

"We're not at home this morning,"
she said.

Rat-a-tat. There it was again. And
again. Whoever it was wouldn't go away.

"They've come to tell me they've found
the train," said Mrs Reid. "Well, I don't
want to know. Not yet, anyway."

Rat-a-tat. "I'll go," said the minister.
"I'll tell them to stay away from here."

He left the room, closing the door

behind him. Alastair heard the front door open and voices, indistinct but raised. "He's really telling them off," he said to himself.

The living room door opened again. The minister stood there. "Look who I've found," he said.

He stood aside. Alastair and his mother gaped in amazement. There stood Alastair's Dad, fit, well and smiling. His cases were at his feet and his arms were spread wide.

★ ★ ★ ★

"It was hearing poor David Mitchell say those words that did it. 'I'm a wee bit feared for the Tay Bridge. I wish I were safe over that rickety concern.' That made me think."

Donald Reid poked at the tobacco in his pipe. Then he said, "The Tay Bridge was still being built when I left for Australia. Well, I'm an engineer and when I looked at it slowly taking shape I must admit I had my doubts. It looked so frail. Even so, I was looking forward to my first trip across it which would bring me home."

He took a long pull on his pipe and clouds of blue tobacco smoke wreathed wound his face. "As my train left the Firth of Forth and drew nearer the Tay, I slept. I dreamt about you, Alastair. You were trying to warn me about something. I woke just as the train drew into St Fort station. I got out of the train to stretch my legs. I spoke to David Mitchell and he said

those words. It was then, Alastair, that I knew what your warning was."

"I had a dream, too," said Alastair.

Donald Reid got up, crossed to the window and looked out.

The water was calm now, silvery and sparkling in winter sunshine. But its new emptiness was a sight to grieve over and they knew they would never forget the great Tay Bridge disaster.

★ ★ ★ ★

The Tay Bridge

The railway races

In the 19th-century, there was ferocious competition between two routes which ran between London and Scotland – one went up the East Coast, and one went up the West.

The East Coast route in England was run by the Great Northern Railway and the North Eastern Railway. Up to the Scottish border, their trains were easily faster. But once in Scotland, their route was broken by two great rivers, the Forth and the Tay, which the passengers crossed by ferries.

Sir Thomas Bouch

The North British Railway Company asked the famous engineer Thomas Bouch to design two bridges, first across the Tay and when that was done, across the Forth.

Unfortunately, the railway

company wanted them done as cheaply as possible. Bouch agreed and said his iron lattices – criss-cross iron strips riveted together – would be both cheaper and stronger than the great slabs of stone and iron in other bridges.

Building the bridge

Things went wrong at once. A survey of the river bed said it was made of hard rock. Only when the first piles were sunk did Bouch find this just wasn't true. He should have stopped work at once and started again. Instead he tried to carry on, propping the piers up with concrete and iron girders.

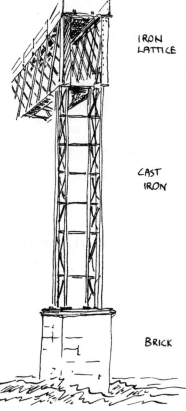

IRON LATTICE

CAST IRON

BRICK

Then, the iron foundries in Dundee refused to do the ironwork for the money they were offered. So Bouch had to set up his own foundries and their work just wasn't good enough. There were tales of girders having splits in them which were filled with cement, bolts sheering through because the holes they went through were too big, joints which didn't fit properly and many other rumours which were kept quiet. Building the bridge was just a story of things going wrong.

Opening day

Even so, when Queen Victoria opened the bridge in 1878, people thought it was a masterpiece – the longest bridge in the world and the most beautiful to look at. And if the Queen herself was happy to cross it in a train, then it must be good. It was a great day for Dundee and for Thomas Bouch.

After the disaster

Nobody could believe what had happened. Divers set to work and found the girders with the train amazingly still inside. The carriages were wrecked – but, incredibly, engine number 224 was hardly damaged. When it was finally recovered, it was repaired and ran for

many years on the North British Railway. But –
except for once just before it was scrapped – it
never again ran over the Tay Bridge. The shock
killed poor Sir Thomas Bouch. He never worked
again and died a year later. Somebody else
designed the new Tay Bridge, which is still there
today, and the Forth Bridge, one of the most
famous bridges in the world.

The story

Except for Alastair and his parents, all the people in
this story are real and every event is described
exactly as it happened. Alastair never had a dream
– but many things just as strange happened. For
example, fifty miles away, at the very moment of
the disaster, two men were driving home in a horse-
drawn trap. Suddenly, one said, "The Tay Bridge is
down. I saw it."

Sparks: Historical Adventures

ANCIENT GREECE
The Great Horse of Troy – The Trojan War
0 7496 3369 7 (hbk)   0 7496 3538 X (pbk)
The Winner's Wreath – Ancient Greek Olympics
0 7496 3368 9 (hbk)   0 7496 3555 X (pbk)

INVADERS AND SETTLERS
Viking Raiders – A Norse Attack
0 7496 3089 2 (hbk)   0 7496 3457 X (pbk)
Boudica Strikes Back – The Romans in Britain
0 7496 3366 2 (hbk)   0 7496 3546 0 (pbk)
Erik's New Home – A Viking Town
0 7496 3367 0 (hbk)   0 7496 3552 5 (pbk)
TALES OF THE ROWDY ROMANS
The Great Necklace Hunt
0 7496 2221 0 (hbk)   0 7496 2628 3 (pbk)
The Lost Legionary
0 7496 2222 9 (hbk)   0 7496 2629 1 (pbk)
The Guard Dog Geese
0 7496 2331 4 (hbk)   0 7496 2630 5 (pbk)
A Runaway Donkey
0 7496 2332 2 (hbk)   0 7496 2631 3 (pbk)

TUDORS AND STUARTS
Captain Drake's Orders – The Armada
0 7496 2556 2 (hbk)   0 7496 3121 X (pbk)
London's Burning – The Great Fire of London
0 7496 2557 0 (hbk)   0 7496 3122 8 (pbk)
Mystery at the Globe – Shakespeare's Theatre
0 7496 3096 5 (hbk)   0 7496 3449 9 (pbk)
Stranger in the Glen – Rob Roy
0 7496 2586 4 (hbk)   0 7496 3123 6 (pbk)
A Dream of Danger – The Massacre of Glencoe
0 7496 2587 2 (hbk)   0 7496 3124 4 (pbk)
A Queen's Promise – Mary Queen of Scots
0 7496 2589 9 (hbk)   0 7496 3125 2 (pbk)
Over the Sea to Skye – Bonnie Prince Charlie
0 7496 2588 0 (hbk)   0 7496 3126 0 (pbk)
Plague! – A Tudor Epidemic
0 7496 3365 4 (hbk)   0 7496 3556 8 (pbk)
TALES OF A TUDOR TEARAWAY
A Pig Called Henry
0 7496 2204 4 (hbk)   0 7496 2625 9 (pbk)
A Horse Called Deathblow
0 7496 2205 9 (hbk)   0 7496 2624 0 (pbk)
Dancing for Captain Drake
0 7496 2234 2 (hbk)   0 7496 2626 7 (pbk)
Birthdays are a Serious Business
0 7496 2235 0 (hbk)   0 7496 2627 5 (pbk)

VICTORIAN ERA
The Runaway Slave – The British Slave Trade
0 7496 3093 0 (hbk)   0 7496 3456 X (pbk)
The Sewer Sleuth – Victorian Cholera
0 7496 2590 2 (hbk)   0 7496 3128 7 (pbk)
Convict! – Criminals Sent to Australia
0 7496 2591 0 (hbk)   0 7496 3129 5 (pbk)
The Great Raj – The British in India
0 7496 3090 6 (hbk)   0 7496 3451 0 (pbk)
Farewell to Ireland – Emigration to America
0 7496 3094 9 (hbk)   0 7496 3448 0 (pbk)
The Great Hunger – Famine in Ireland
0 7496 3095 7 (hbk)   0 7496 3447 2 (pbk)
Fire Down the Pit – A Welsh Mining Disaster
0 7496 3091 4 (hbk)   0 7496 3450 2 (pbk)
Tunnel Rescue – The Great Western Railway
0 7496 3353 0 (hbk)   0 7496 3537 1 (pbk)
Kidnap on the Canal – Victorian Waterways
0 7496 3352 2 (hbk)   0 7496 3540 1 (pbk)
Dr. Barnardo's Boys – Victorian Charity
0 7496 3358 1 (hbk)   0 7496 3541 X (pbk)
The Iron Ship – Brunel's Great Britain
0 7496 3355 7 (hbk)   0 7496 3543 6 (pbk)
Bodies for Sale – Victorian Tomb-Robbers
0 7496 3364 6 (hbk)   0 7496 3539 8 (pbk)
Penny Post Boy – The Victorian Postal Service
0 7496 3362 X (hbk)   0 7496 3544 4 (pbk)
The Canal Diggers – The Manchester Ship Canal
0 7496 3356 5 (hbk)   0 7496 3545 2 (pbk)
The Tay Bridge Tragedy – A Victorian Disaster
0 7496 3354 9 (hbk)   0 7496 3547 9 (pbk)
Stop, Thief! – The Victorian Police
0 7496 3359 X (hbk)   0 7496 3548 7 (pbk)
Miss Buss and Miss Beale – Victorian Schools
0 7496 3360 3 (hbk)   0 7496 3549 5 (pbk)
Chimney Charlie – Victorian Chimney Sweeps
0 7496 3351 4 (hbk)   0 7496 3551 7 (pbk)
Down the Drain – Victorian Sewers
0 7496 3357 3 (hbk)   0 7496 3550 9 (pbk)
The Ideal Home – A Victorian New Town
0 7496 3361 1 (hbk)   0 7496 3553 3 (pbk)
Stage Struck – Victorian Music Hall
0 7496 3363 8 (hbk)   0 7496 3554 1 (pbk)
TRAVELS OF A YOUNG VICTORIAN
The Golden Key
0 7496 2360 8 (hbk)   0 7496 2632 1 (pbk)
Poppy's Big Push
0 7496 2361 6 (hbk)   0 7496 2633 X (pbk)
Poppy's Secret
0 7496 2374 8 (hbk)   0 7496 2634 8 (pbk)
The Lost Treasure
0 7496 2375 6 (hbk)   0 7496 2635 6 (pbk)

20th-CENTURY HISTORY
Fight for the Vote – The Suffragettes
0 7496 3092 2 (hbk)   0 7496 3452 9 (pbk)
The Road to London – The Jarrow March
0 7496 2609 7 (hbk)   0 7496 3132 5 (pbk)
The Sandbag Secret – The Blitz
0 7496 2608 9 (hbk)   0 7496 3133 3 (pbk)
Sid's War – Evacuation
0 7496 3209 7 (hbk)   0 7496 3445 6 (pbk)
D-Day! – Wartime Adventure
0 7496 3208 9 (hbk)   0 7496 3446 4 (pbk)
The Prisoner – A Prisoner of War
0 7496 3212 7 (hbk)   0 7496 3455 3 (pbk)
Escape from Germany – Wartime Refugees
0 7496 3211 9 (hbk)   0 7496 3454 5 (pbk)
Flying Bombs – Wartime Bomb Disposal
0 7496 3210 0 (hbk)   0 7496 3453 7 (pbk)
12,000 Miles From Home – Sent to Australia
0 7496 3370 0 (hbk) 0 7496 3542 8 (pbk)